MAR 1 8 2008

Why COWGIRLS Are Such Sweet Talkers

JmRice

Why COWGIRLS Are Such Sweet Talkers

Written by Laurie Lazzaro Knowlton

Illustrated by James Rice

PELICAN PUBLISHING COMPANY
Gretna 2000

RETA E. KING LIBRARY
CHADRON STATE COLLEGE
CHADRON, NE 69337

Copyright © 2000
By Laurie Lazzaro Knowlton

Illustrations copyright © 2000
By James Rice
All rights reserved

Let your conversation be always full of Grace, seasoned with salt, so that you may know how to answer everyone. (Col. 4:6)

For my Creator and for my daughters, Charlotte and Kelsey

The word "Pelican" and the depiction of a pelican are trademarks of Pelican Publishing Company, Inc., and are registered in the U.S. Patent and Trademark Office.

Library of Congress Cataloging-in-Publication Data

Knowlton, Laurie Lazzaro.
Why cowgirls are such sweet talkers / by Laurie Lazzaro Knowlton ; illustrated by James Rice.
p. cm.
Summary: Gabby the cowgirl shows everyone that kind words to man or beast can have very positive results for everyone.
ISBN: 1-56554-698-9 (hc : alk. paper)
[1. Cowboys—Fiction. 2. Ranch life—Fiction. 3. Behavior—Fiction.] I. Rice, James, 1934- ill. II. Title.

PZ7.K7685 Wj 2000
[Fic]—dc21 99-054655

Printed in Hong Kong

Published by Pelican Publishing Company, Inc.
1000 Burmaster Street, Gretna, Louisiana 70053

+E
K767wc

WHY COWGIRLS ARE SUCH SWEET TALKERS

Cowgirl Gabby was one sweet-talking gal. She talked to the fellers. She talked to her horse. Why, she could talk the hide off a cow. Nobody seemed to mind much, 'cause in those parts women were scarcer than whiskers on a rattler.

6-30-01 Long Rider 14.95

One day Gabby and her pardner, Slim Jim Watkins, came across a cowhand and his mule. That cowhand was screeching at that mule like a blue jay being robbed of a meal.

"You better get moving or I'm taking you to the glue factory!" he yelled.

“That’s no way to talk to your pardner here.” Gabby patted the mule. “If you want him to move all you have to do is sweet-talk him.”

“Sweet-talk a mule? Have you gone plumb loco?”

Cowgirl Gabby just smiled and whispered in that mule’s ear.

RETA E. KING LIBRARY
CHADRON STATE COLLEGE
CHADRON, NE 69337

“Well, I’ll be!” said Slim Jim Watkins. “What did you say to him?”

“I just sweet-talked him.” Gabby gave that mule a pat and then she and Slim rode off.

At the corral where Gabby practiced her trick riding, a cowboy was picking himself off the ground. The cowboy rubbed his backside as if he was polishing his boots for courting.

"That horse is jumpy as popcorn in a skillet."

Gabby looked that cowhand over and said, "No one likes getting poked. Why don't you try riding him without the spurs? And a little sweet talking wouldn't hurt none either."

"Sweet-talk Tornado? Have you gone plumb loco?"

Cowgirl Gabby just smiled and whispered in Tornado's ear.

RETA E KING LIBRARY
CHADRON STATE COLLEGE
CHADRON, NE 69337

“Well, I’ll be!” said Slim Jim Watkins. “What did you say to him?”
“I just sweet-talked him and rode without poking him.” Gabby gave Tornado a pat and she was off to practice her trick riding.

JMRice

Later that evening, Gabby heard more commotion than a chuck wagon on a frozen trail coming from the cowhands' bunkhouse. The next thing you know, out rolled a drugstore cowboy. He was redder than a chili pepper. All the cowhands laughed it up like a bunch of hyenas.

"Funning with the new cowhand, I see." Gabby gave the cowboy a hand up.

"That ain't no cowhand. That's a greenhorn!" said one of the cowboys. All the cowhands laughed.

“Is that so?” asked Gabby. “Seems to me you had trouble sitting on a horse for more than three seconds when you first got here. And, Joe, how many times did you get tangled up in your rope before I showed you how?”

"And, Patches, who was it got you out of those holey pants and into a pair of britches you wouldn't bust out of?"

"Now just a minute, Gabby," said Patches. "There's no reason to get personal here. All we're doing is having a little fun trying to make him a real cowboy!"

Well, Gabby looked that cowhand over and said, "The only way I know to make a greenhorn a cowboy is to give him a hand and sweet-talk him."

"Sweet-talk a greenhorn? Have you gone plumb loco?"

Cowgirl Gabby just smiled and whispered in that greenhorn's ear.

CHADRON STATE COLL
CHADRON, NE 69337

JMRICE

“Well, I’ll be!” said the cowboys. “What did you say to him?”

"I just sweet-talked him without funning him none." Gabby gave that cowboy a pat on the back and he stood just as tall as a steeple on a church. Then Gabby was on her way.

"Aw shucks, Slim, you know the words are just honey on a biscuit. It's the doing that says it all."

"You mean like this?" Slim handed Gabby a flower and whispered in her ear.

Cowgirl Gabby just smiled and said, "Why, Slim Jim Watkins, you sweet talker you!"

Slim Jim Watkins scratched his head and said, “Hey, Gabby, come on and tell me. What did you say to that feller, anyway?”